The Magic Porridge Pot

Jackie Walter and Anna C. Leplar

Once upon a time, there was a poor girl who lived with her mother. They never had much money and they were often hungry. One day, all they had to eat was a small crust of bread.

The next morning, the girl sat and cried. She was so hungry. Her mother had gone to look for food.

Suddenly, an old lady appeared.

"Whatever is the matter, dear?"

she asked the girl kindly.

The girl looked up into the old lady's smiling face. "I'm hungry," she replied. "Mother and I never have enough food to eat."

"Well, I can help with that! With this pot, you shall never be hungry again," said the old lady. She took out a small, shiny pot.

"You see, this little pot is magic!" the old lady explained. "Whenever you are hungry, just say to the pot: 'Cook, little pot, cook!' and it will cook you all the porridge you could ever want."

The girl could hardly believe her ears.

"When you have enough porridge," the old lady added, "just say: 'Stop, little pot, stop!' and the pot will stop cooking."

"Thank you!" said the girl, who was smiling at last.

The girl took the pot indoors. She put it on the table and waited for her mother to return. She could not wait to show her mother the magic pot.

"Cook, little pot, cook!" the girl said when her mother had sat down. And the pot cooked delicious porridge until the girl said: "Stop, little pot, stop!" The girl's mother could hardly believe her eyes!

The whole family ate delicious porridge for many weeks and quickly forgot how hungry they had been. The girl and her mother had never been so happy.

Then, one day, the girl went out to take her dog for a walk.

The mother was feeling a little hungry,
so she said: "Cook, little pot, cook!"

The pot cooked the delicious porridge
as usual.

The mother sat down to enjoy her lunch. But she forgot to tell the little pot to stop cooking!

When the mother had finished, she looked around. She was shocked to see a puddle of porridge on the floor!

But she could not remember how to tell the pot to stop, and the magic little pot kept on cooking.

Soon the porridge filled the house.
It pushed the door open and spilled
on to the street. The mother ran from
the house with the porridge puddle
following her. Still the magic little pot

kept on cooking.

23

The porridge puddle flowed through the school and glugged into the children's playground.

The children happily splashed and sploshed in the porridge. Still the magic little pot kept on cooking.

When the girl returned, she saw her mother on the roof, just above the sea of porridge.

"Quick!" shouted her mother. "Make the pot stop cooking!"

"Stop, little pot, stop!" yelled the girl.
The magic little pot stopped cooking
at last.

The villagers fetched their spoons and had a porridge party. It lasted a long, long time!

About the story

The Little Porridge Pot is also known by the name *Sweet Porridge.* It is a fairy tale from Germany. The story was published by the Brothers Grimm in 1812. The story can be seen as having different morals: knowing how to finish something before you start it and that you can have too much of a good thing. A warning against magic you cannot control is also a popular theme in stories – even today.

Be in the story!

Imagine you are
the little girl.
How do you feel when
you see your mother
sitting on the roof?

Now imagine you
are the mother.
How do you feel
when your little
girl finally returns
home?

Franklin Watts
First published in Great Britain in 2015 by The Watts Publishing Group

Copyright © The Watts Publishing Group 2015

The rights of Jackie Walter to be identified as the author
and Anna C. Leplar to be identified as the illustrator
of this Work have been asserted in accordance with the
Copyright, Designs and Patents Act, 1988.

Series Editor: Jackie Hamley
Series Advisor: Catherine Glavina
Series Designer: Cathryn Gilbert

A CIP catalogue record for this book is available
from the British Library.

The artwork for this story first appeared in
Leapfrog Fairy Tales: The Magic Porridge Pot

ISBN 978 1 4451 4448 1 (hbk)
ISBN 978 1 4451 4450 4 (pbk)
ISBN 978 1 4451 4449 8 (library ebook)
ISBN 978 1 4451 4451 1 (ebook)

Printed in China

Franklin Watts
An imprint of
Hachette Children's Group
Part of The Watts Publishing Group
Carmelite House
50 Victoria Embankment
London EC4Y 0DZ

An Hachette UK Company
www.hachette.co.uk

www.franklinwatts.co.uk

FSC
www.fsc.org
MIX
Paper from
responsible sources
FSC® C104740